P9-BXX-914

Disney

TIM BURTON'S

THE NIGHTMARE BEFORE CHRISTMAS

ZERO'S JOURNEY

BOOK ONE

WRITTEN BY
D.J. MILKY

MAIN PRINTING COVER BY
KIYOSHI ARAI

VARIANT COVER BY
CAMILLA D'ERRICO

STORYBOARDS AND PENCILS BY
KEI ISHIYAMA

INKS BY
DAVID HUTCHISON

COLORS BY
DAN CONNER

CONTENTS

◇◇◇◇◇◇◇◇◇◇◇◇◇◇◇◇◇◇◇◇◇◇◇◇◇◇◇◇

FOREWORD

DEAR FELLOW NIGHTMARIANS:

TOGETHER WE JOURNEY THROUGH A WHIMSICAL WORLD CREATED BY TIM BURTON! LUCKY FOR ALL OF US, WE'VE GOT OUR TRUSTY HOUND ZERO BY OUR SIDE. BUT WAIT! MISCHIEVOUS ZERO - WHERE'D HE DISAPPEAR TO THIS TIME?!

HOW MANY OF YOU RECALL WATCHING THE LEGENDARY MOVIE AND WISHING YOU COULD PLAY CATCH WITH ZERO, PET HIM AND GO FOR A WALK WITH THE PUP? OR AT LEAST SEE HIM IN A FEW MORE SCENES...

WELL, WE'VE GOT ZERO FOR YOU - AND HE'S OUR STAR! IF ONLY POOR JACK COULD FIND HIM...

JOIN US ON THIS MAGICAL JOURNEY, EXPLORING THE NOOKS AND CRANNIES OF CHRISTMAS TOWN, TOGETHER WITH ZERO - AND MEETING SOME QUIRKY FUN CHARACTERS ALONG THE WAY.

THIS SPECIAL GRAPHIC NOVEL COLLECTS ISSUES 0 THROUGH 4 OF ***THE NIGHTMARE BEFORE CHRISTMAS: ZERO'S JOURNEY*** COMIC - THE FIRST OF FOUR SUCH GRAPHIC NOVELS. HERE AT TOKYOPOP, WE COULDN'T BE PROUDER TO BRING IT TO YOU, CREATED BY SUCH A TALENTED INTERNATIONAL TEAM OF ALCHEMISTS.

WE'D LOVE TO HEAR FROM YOU, WITH YOUR IMPRESSIONS, FEEDBACK, AND EVEN RHYTHMIC NONSENSE. AFTER ALL, WE'RE ALL NIGHTMARIANS TOGETHER.

THIS IS CHRISTMAS!

—TEAM TOKYOPOP

HALLOWEEN TOWN, JACK SKELLINGTON'S ABODE
SNIFFLE
SNORE
SNORE
ZERO

HMM...
I JUST CAN'T SEEM TO GET IT RIGHT...
I WONDER WHAT THE PROBLEM IS...

BOING
I'VE GOT THE PORTAL UP AND OPERATING--
BUT WHY WON'T IT NAVIGATE PROPERLY?!
WOOF
RING...
ZERO!
NOT NOW, I'M TRYING TO CONCENTRATE.
RING...

HELLO?
AH, MR. MAYOR.
JACK, MAKING PROGRESS?
JACK!!
HOW DID YOU FAIR?
I JUST CAN'T WAIT TO SEE YOUR SCARES!
NOT QUITE READY, MR. MAYOR.
I NEED MORE TIME.
CLICK

IF I CAN'T SOLVE THIS...
MY BIG PLANS WILL BE RUINED!
...
OPEN
CLOSE
MAYBE DR. FINKLESTEIN CAN HELP ME AGAIN.
CREAK
I'M SO CLOSE TO REACHING ALL THE HOLIDAYS -- THE WHOLE WORLD!

NUDGE
NUDGE
ZOOM
WOOF
POP
WOOF
JUST FOR A BIT, ZERO!

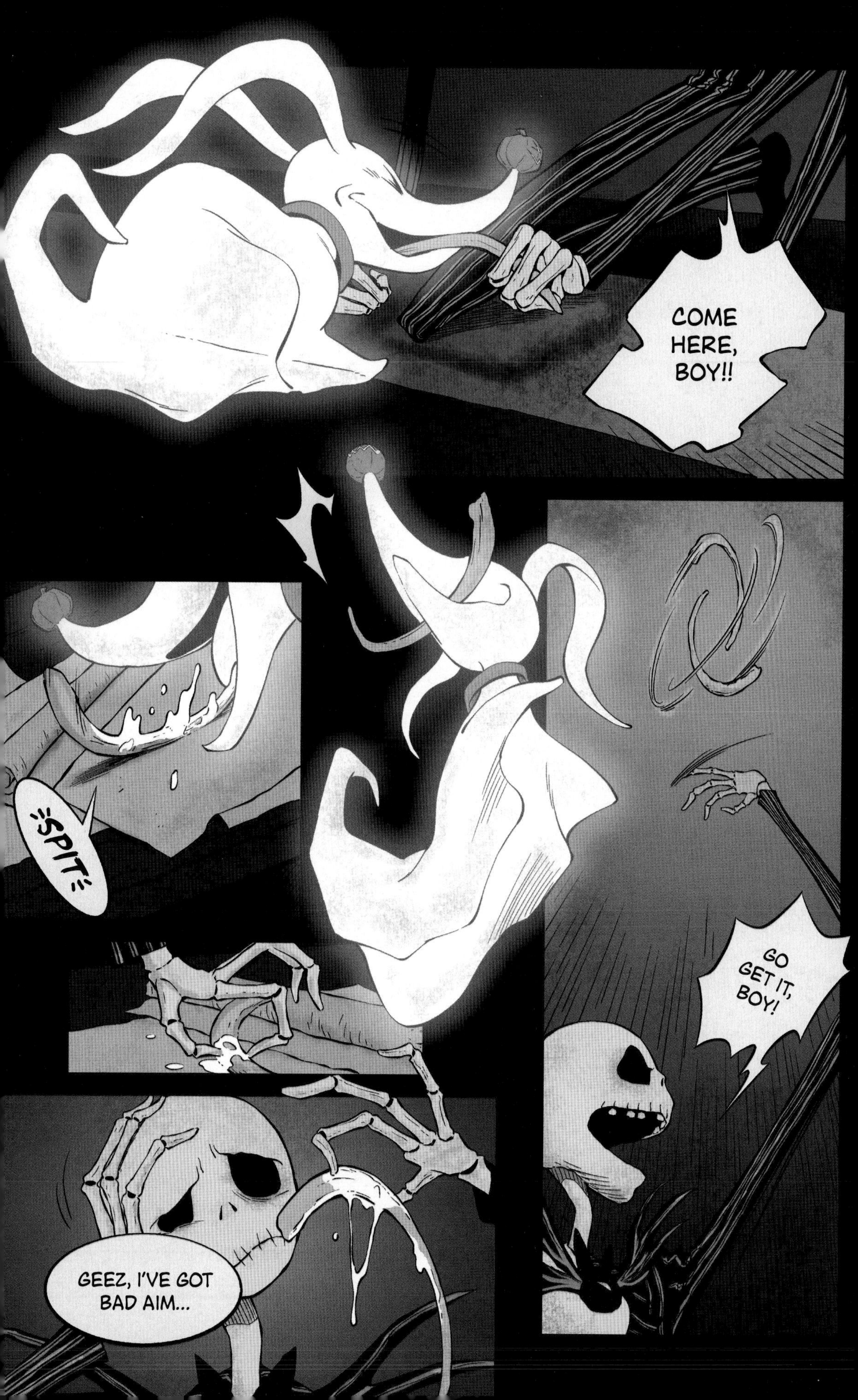
COME HERE, BOY!!
SPIT
GO GET IT, BOY!
GEEZ, I'VE GOT BAD AIM...

WOOF
OVER THERE, GO GET IT!
THUD
BAM

CAREFUL, ZERO -- THAT STUFF'S IMPORTANT!
ZERO...
NO MORE...
WRIGGLE
WRIGGLE
WOOF

OH, ZERO...
LIFE IS SO EASY FOR YOU...
PANT
PANT
WOOF
LAST ONE, ZERO!

SLAP
WHOOPS!
OPEN
CLOSE
BUMP

WHOA WHOA!
WOOF
BEEP
WHIRR
WHIRR
WHIRR
H-SSSSSSSSSSSSSS

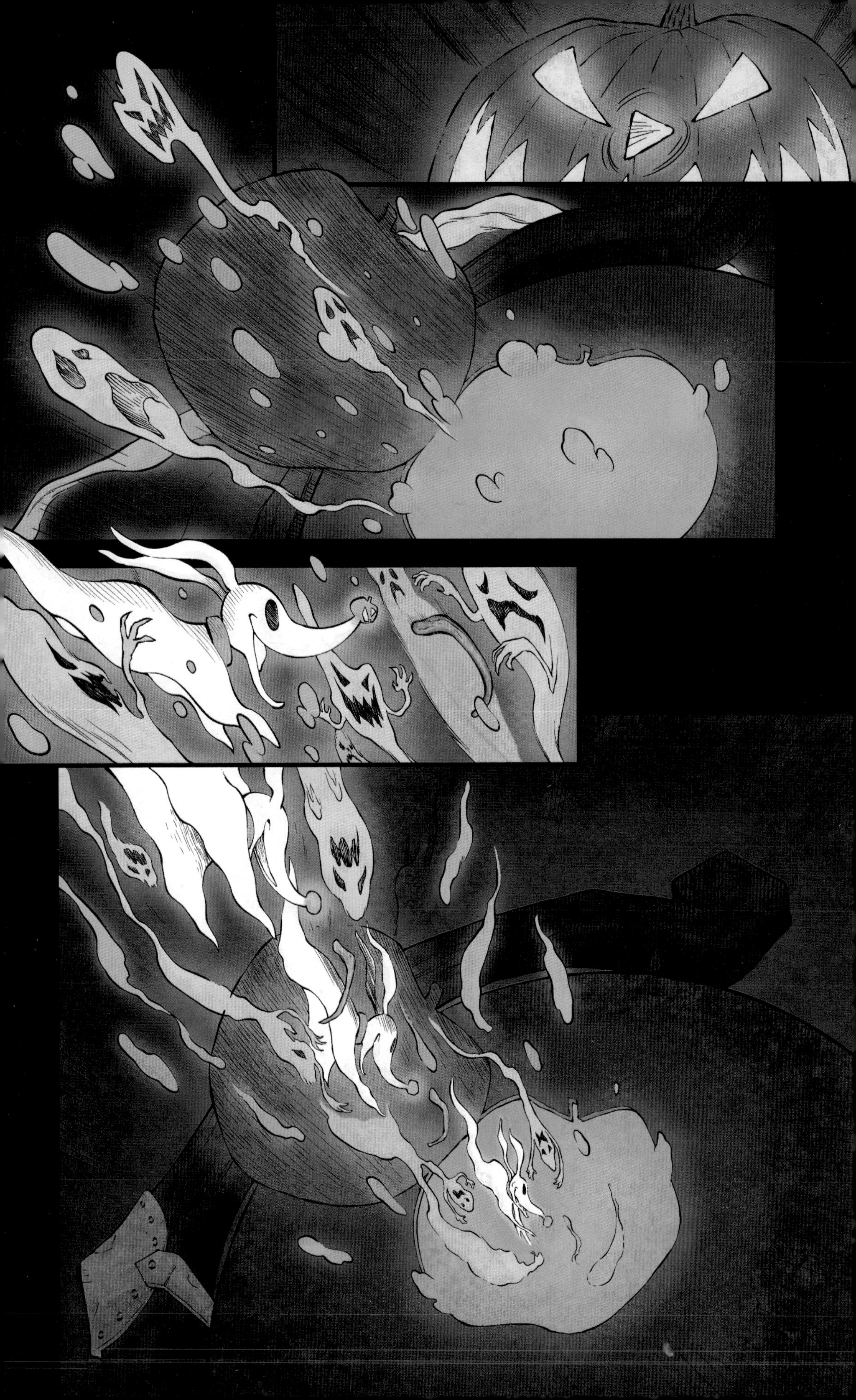

ZERO -- NO!!!
AH!
OPEN
CLOSE
ZERO...
...!!
RUMBLE
RUMBLE

FLASH
WOOF
WOOF
WOOF

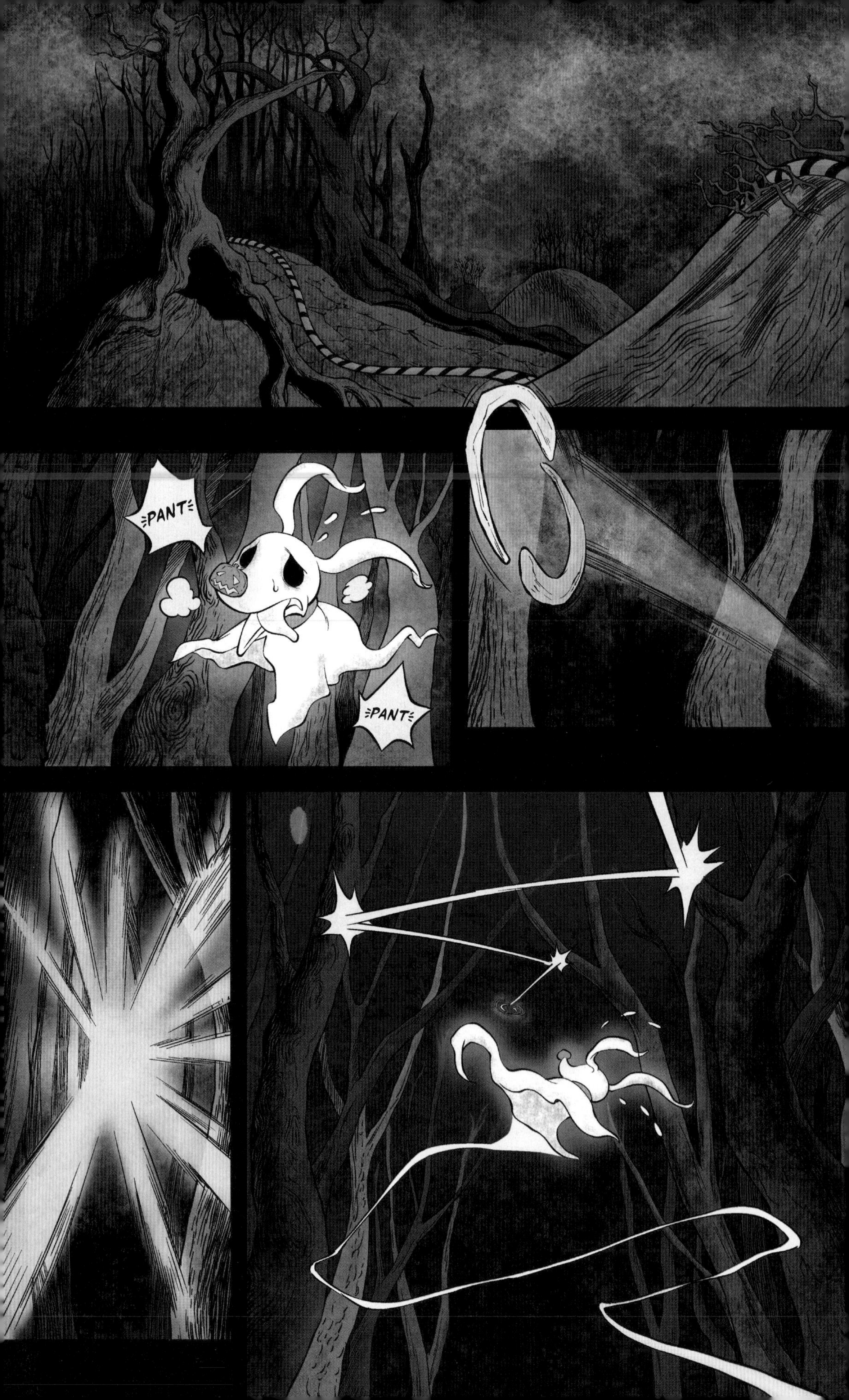
PANT
PANT

THUNK
CLICK
THUNK

SNIFF
SNIFF
TWINKLE
TWINKLE

SLAM
WOOOF!

WHOOSH
FUMP

WHOOSH
SLAM
SHAKE
SHAKE

...
TAP
TAP

HOOOOT.

FLAP
HOO-HOO.

WOOF
WOOF
TILT
BLINK
...

...
HOP
SNIFF
TUG
TUG
WOOF

HOO-HOOT!
FLAP

CHRISTMAS TOWN

CHRISTMAS TOWN

WHEEE!
WHIRL
WHIRL
HAHAHA!

TROT
TROT
TROT

LOOK AT YOU...
POOR THING!

LICK
LICK
DRINK.
YOU MUST BE THIRSTY!
TASTY, ISN'T IT?
SLURP
SLURP
PUMPKIN SPICE MIXED WITH EGG NOG, WHO WOULDN'T LOVE IT?
WOW!

COME, LITTLE ONE.
YOU MUST BE TIRED.
AWWW.
SO HUNGRY!
THERE, THERE.
SO, YOU HAVE COME FROM ANOTHER TOWN?
TRAVELED FAR, EH?

BEING A GHOST DOG AND ALL, YOU MUST COME FROM THE TOWN OF HALLOWEEN, EH?
WOOF WOOF
WOOF
HOWLY BROUGHT YOU HERE BECAUSE...
YOU CANNOT FIND YOUR WAY HOME.
HOWLY.
THE BOOK, PLEASE.
GLOW
FLAP

PURR
THANK YOU.
CHRISTMAS
CHRISTMAS
NOW THIS, YOUNG DOGGY...
... IS THE BOOK OF CHRISTMAS.
IT SHOWS OUR MANY TRADITIONS.
I THINK YOU'LL ENJOY IT.

CHRISTMAS
FLIP
CHRISTMAS TOWN IS A JOYOUS PLACE.
CRACKLE
CRACKLE
BARK!
LOOK AT THIS BOOK, DOGGY, AND LET ME EXPLAIN...

"WINTER, WINTER, WINTER."
"WE LOVE THE FLUFFY WHITE STUFF CALLED SNOW!"
"WINTER, WINTER, WINTER."
"START WITH SOME DROPS... THEN WATCH HOW THEY GROW!"

JUST LIKE YOUR HOLIDAY HALLOWEEN--
OUR CHRISTMAS HAPPENS ONLY ONCE A YEAR.
"WINTER, WINTER, WINTER."
"OUR TIME OF YEAR IS KNOWN FOR THE COLD."
"WINTER, WINTER, WINTER."
"WE SING LOUD AND BOLD."
"WE DON'T HIDE AWAY..."

"WINTER WONDERLAND,
WINTER WONDERLAND!"
"REINDEER FLYING BY,
ON A SLEIGH RIDE IN
THE SKY."

Previously in Halloween Town...
...

NOW THIS IS SANTA CLAUS.
NOT *SANDY CLAWS* LIKE YOUR PEOPLE BELIEVE.
"WINTER WONDERLAND, WINTER WONDERLAND."
"SANTA WITH HIS SACK, PRESENTS FULLY PACKED."

EASTER
HALLOWEEN
EASTER
MORE FUN THAN EASTER--
AND WE DON'T MEAN TO BE MEAN...
HALLOWEEN
... BUT EVEN ALL THE CHILDREN LOVE US--
MORE THAN HALLOWEEN!

WOOF
WOOF
BOOK of HALLOWEEN
HALLOWEEN
WE'RE CERTAIN YOU'LL HAVE FOUND--
THAT YOU'RE EVER SO LUCKY TO BE LOST IN CHRISTMAS TOWN!
PPPOUUT

BUT WAIT!
YOU'RE NOT CONVINCED?
...
IT SEEMS YOU DON'T WANT TO STAY...
CRACKLE
CRACKLE

WE DON'T KNOW EXACTLY WHERE THE DOORS OF HOLIDAY ARE LOCATED IN OUR FOREST--

BUT WE CAN USUALLY SPOT THEM WHILE WE FLY DURING A FULL MOON.

THIS YEAR, CHRISTMAS EVE FALLS ON A FULL MOON.
I THINK IT MAY BE YOUR BEST CHANCE TO FIND HOME.

IF WE ASK SANTA FOR PERMISSION--
PERHAPS HE WOULD LET YOU JOIN THIS YEAR'S RIDE?
THAT WAY, FROM THE SKY, YOU CAN LOOK FOR THE DOOR TO HALLOWEEN TOWN.

WOOF
SPIN
CHRISTMAS IS ONLY ONE WEEK AWAY, SO THE TIMING IS GOOD.
WE WILL ASK SANTA.

"WINTER WONDERLAND, WINTER WONDERLAND."
FLIP
"TREETOPS LIKE TO GLISTEN..."
"BELLS THAT LIKE TO JINGLE..."
"WHEN CHIMES ARE HEARD ACROSS THE TOWN, PEOPLE LIKE TO LISTEN!"

"SCRUMPTIOUS CAKES AND COOKIES CUT IN SHAPES!"
"CINNAMON AND NUTMEG TREASURES OVEN-BAKED."
"WINTER WONDERLAND, WINTER WONDERLAND."

"MELODIC VOICES SINGING CAROLS FOR YOU TO HEAR."
"ON EVERY DOOR WREATHS OF HOLLY DO APPEAR."
"WARMING UP BY THE FIRE WITH YOUR DEAR."
"ROASTED CHESTNUTS AND CUPS OF EGG NOG FILLED WITH CHEER!"

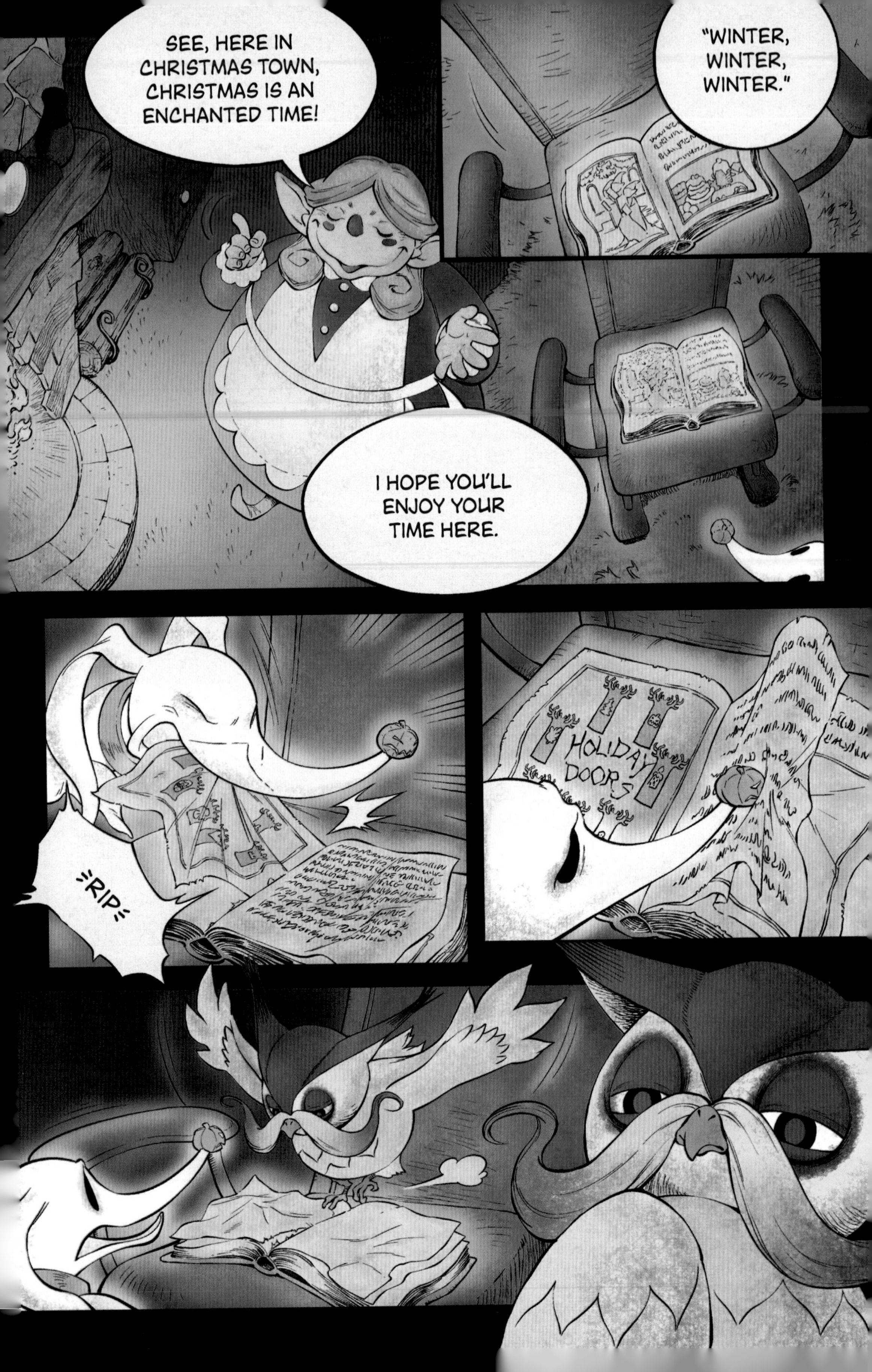
SEE, HERE IN CHRISTMAS TOWN, CHRISTMAS IS AN ENCHANTED TIME!
"WINTER, WINTER, WINTER."
I HOPE YOU'LL ENJOY YOUR TIME HERE.
RIP
HOLIDAY DOORS

SLIDE
YANK
BARK!

WOOF
WOOF

Halloween Town
HE'S GONE!
IT CAN'T BE!
WHERE DID ZERO GO?
ZE

HE'S MISSING!
HE'S GONE!
RUFFLE
RUFFLE
SAY IT ISN'T SO!

STAGGER
MY LITTLE FAITHFUL FOLLOWER!
CLANG
MY GHOSTLY FURRY FRIEND.
I CAN'T BELIEVE I'VE LOST YOU.
COULD THIS BE THE END?

SORRY, JACK...
PROFESSOR.
HAVE YOU SEEN LITTLE ZERO?
I'VE BEEN SO CRUEL--
--IGNORING YOUR NEEDS FOR LOVE!

I'LL SEARCH HIGH!
I'LL SEARCH LOW...
FROM ABOVE,
FROM BELOW!

DEAR JACK...
...YOU SEEM UPSET.
MY LOYAL PUP ZERO...

MURMUR
WE'LL FIND HIM, JACK.
MURMUR
AHEM
AHEM
YOU ALL LOVE JACK!
AFTER ALL, HE IS OUR PUMPKIN KING!
MAYOR

LONG DIE, THE PUMPKIN KING!
YAY, JACK!
WE LOVE YOU, JACK!
BUT NOW JACK NEEDS YOUR HELP!
EVERYONE REMEMBERS JACK'S BEST FRIEND, ZERO.
ZERO HAS GONE MISSING!

EVERYONE IN OUR TOWN MUST HELP FIND ZERO!
YESSSS!!
OH, NO! POOR JACK!
POOR ZERO!
THANK YOU FOR ALL OF YOUR COMPASSION.
CLANG
CLANG
THE SEARCH BEGINS!

GOT TO FIND HIM FOR JACK!
SEARCHING!
WE'RE SEARCHING!
SEARCHING!
WE'RE SEARCHING!
IN THE CREEPY SPIDER WEB!
WILL HIS DOGGY EVER COME BACK?
SEARCHING!
WE'RE SEARCHING!

IN THE GRAVES OF THE DEAD!
SEARCHING.
WE'RE SEARCHING!
CREAK
SEARCHING!
I'M SEARCHING, FOR MY BELOVED DEAR.
WE'RE SEARCHING, SO FAR AND SO NEAR!
SEARCHING!
SLAM

OH, NO!
I MAY BE LOST TOO...
HM?

OH, DARLING JACK.
THIS MAY EXPLAIN IT.
SQUEAK
LOOK WHAT I'VE FOUND...
WOOOOOOF!
WOOF
WHY?
YES.
THAT'S HIS BARK!
IT'S ZERO, YOUR HOUND!

JACK!!
SALLY?

I FOUND HIM!
HE WENT DOWN THE ABYSS--
--INTO CHRISTMAS TOWN!
WHAT?! CHRISTMAS TOWN??
THIS IS TROUBLE!
THAT NASTY SANDY CLAWS...

THERE'S NO CHOICE!
I WILL VISIT CHRISTMAS TOWN TO BRING ZERO HOME!
WHAT DO WE DO?
WOO-HOO!
ALRIGHT, JACK!
YOU CAN DO IT, JACK!

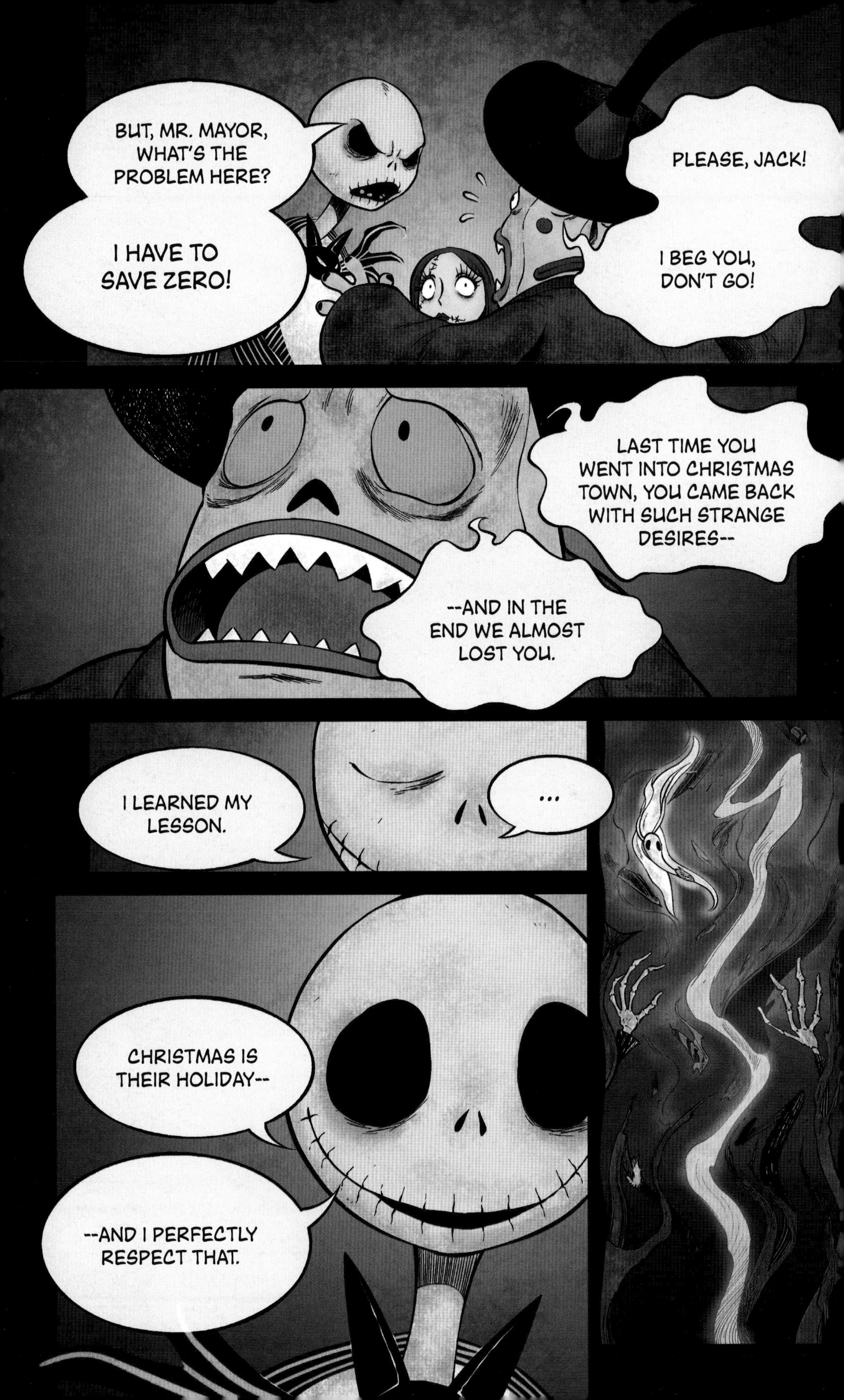
BUT, MR. MAYOR, WHAT'S THE PROBLEM HERE?
I HAVE TO SAVE ZERO!
PLEASE, JACK!
I BEG YOU, DON'T GO!
LAST TIME YOU WENT INTO CHRISTMAS TOWN, YOU CAME BACK WITH SUCH STRANGE DESIRES--
--AND IN THE END WE ALMOST LOST YOU.
I LEARNED MY LESSON.
...
CHRISTMAS IS THEIR HOLIDAY--
--AND I PERFECTLY RESPECT THAT.

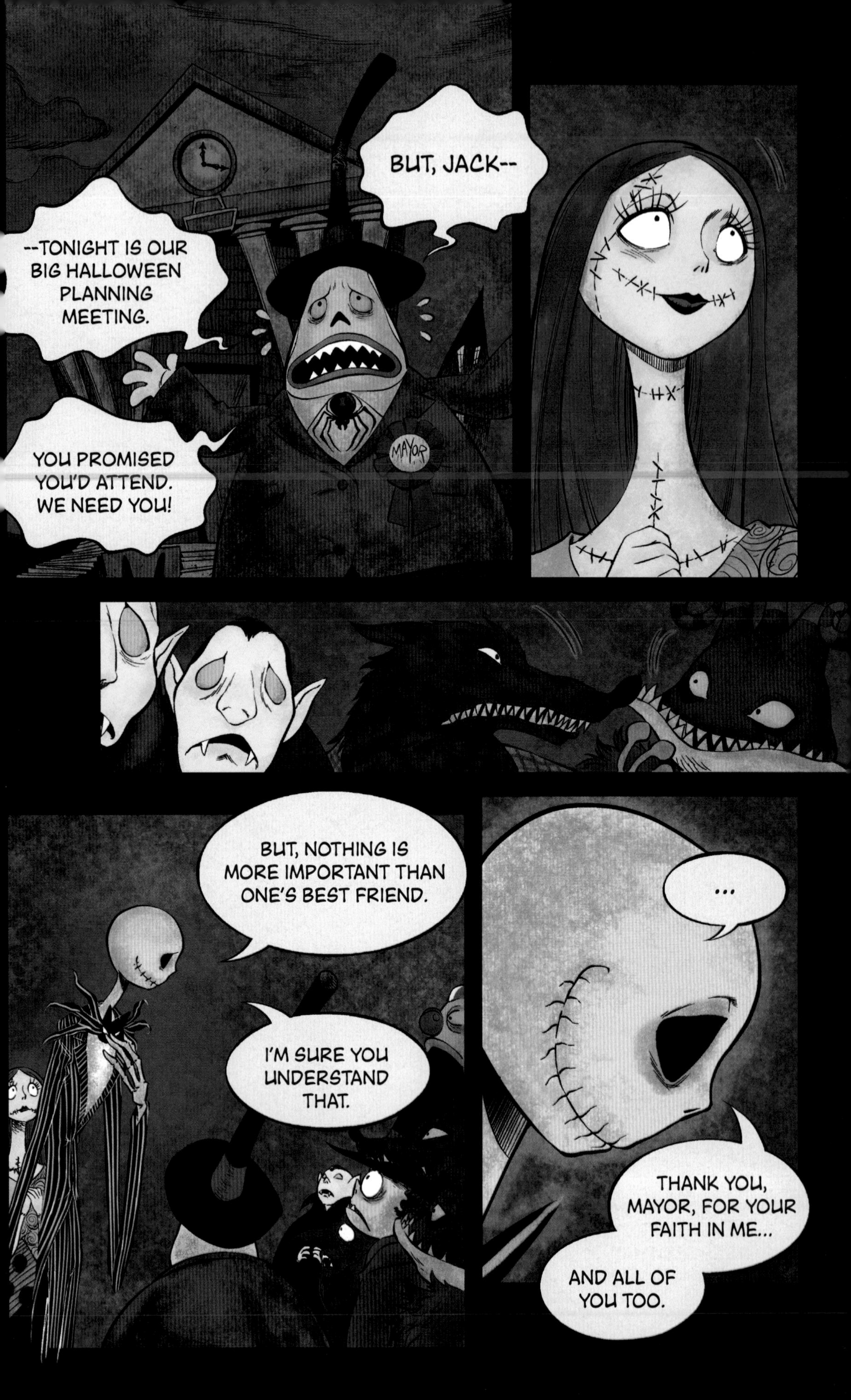
--TONIGHT IS OUR BIG HALLOWEEN PLANNING MEETING.
YOU PROMISED YOU'D ATTEND. WE NEED YOU!
BUT, JACK--
MAYOR
BUT, NOTHING IS MORE IMPORTANT THAN ONE'S BEST FRIEND.
I'M SURE YOU UNDERSTAND THAT.
...
THANK YOU, MAYOR, FOR YOUR FAITH IN ME...
AND ALL OF YOU TOO.

LET US GO!
WE'LL DO IT!
YOU CAN COUNT ON US!
OF COURSE, JACK.
BUT MAYBE SOMEONE CAN GO SEARCH FOR ZERO INSTEAD OF YOU...
WE *ALSO* LEARNED OUR LESSON, JACK!!
OOGIE BOOGIE'S LONG GONE!
WE'LL REDEEM OURSELVES!
THE LAST TIME I RELIED ON YOU TROUBLE-MAKERS--
--YOU HANDED SANDY CLAWS OVER TO OOGIE BOOGIE!
HOW DO I KNOW YOU THREE WON'T CAUSE MISCHIEF AGAIN?
AND WHAT IF YOU DON'T FIND HIM SO EASILY?

WE KNOW CHRISTMAS TOWN BETTER THAN ANYONE!
LET US MAKE IT UP TO YOU!
YOU CAN COUNT ON US.
WELL, I GUESS IT DOES MAKE SENSE...
JACK, THIS IS A PERFECT SOLUTION!
YOU CAN JOIN OUR CRITICAL PLANNING MEETING TONIGHT!
YOU'LL GO STRAIGHT TO ZERO AND NOT GET DISTRACTED BY ANYTHING ELSE?!
WE PROMISE!!!

CHRISTMAS TOWN

WOOF
WOOF

IT'S FLOATING!
LOOK AT THAT WEIRD DOG!
IS IT A... GHOST?
LET'S GET IT!

SLIPPP
!!!
MAYBE HE CAN SKATE TOO!
LET'S SEE IF HE CAN SLIDE!
SCRAMBLE
NO, HE'S HAVING FUN!
HEY, THAT'S MEAN...
CRASH
I DON'T THINK HE LIKED IT...

PANT
PANT
CHOMP

MANGY MUTT!
HEY, YOU!
STOP THAT!
GET OUT OF HERE!
IF I CATCH YOU AGAIN, YOU'LL REGRET IT!

WHIFF
WHIFF
SNEAK

CRASH
THUD

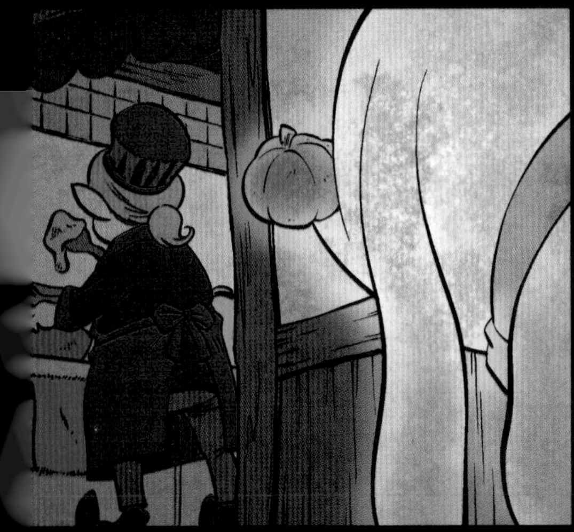

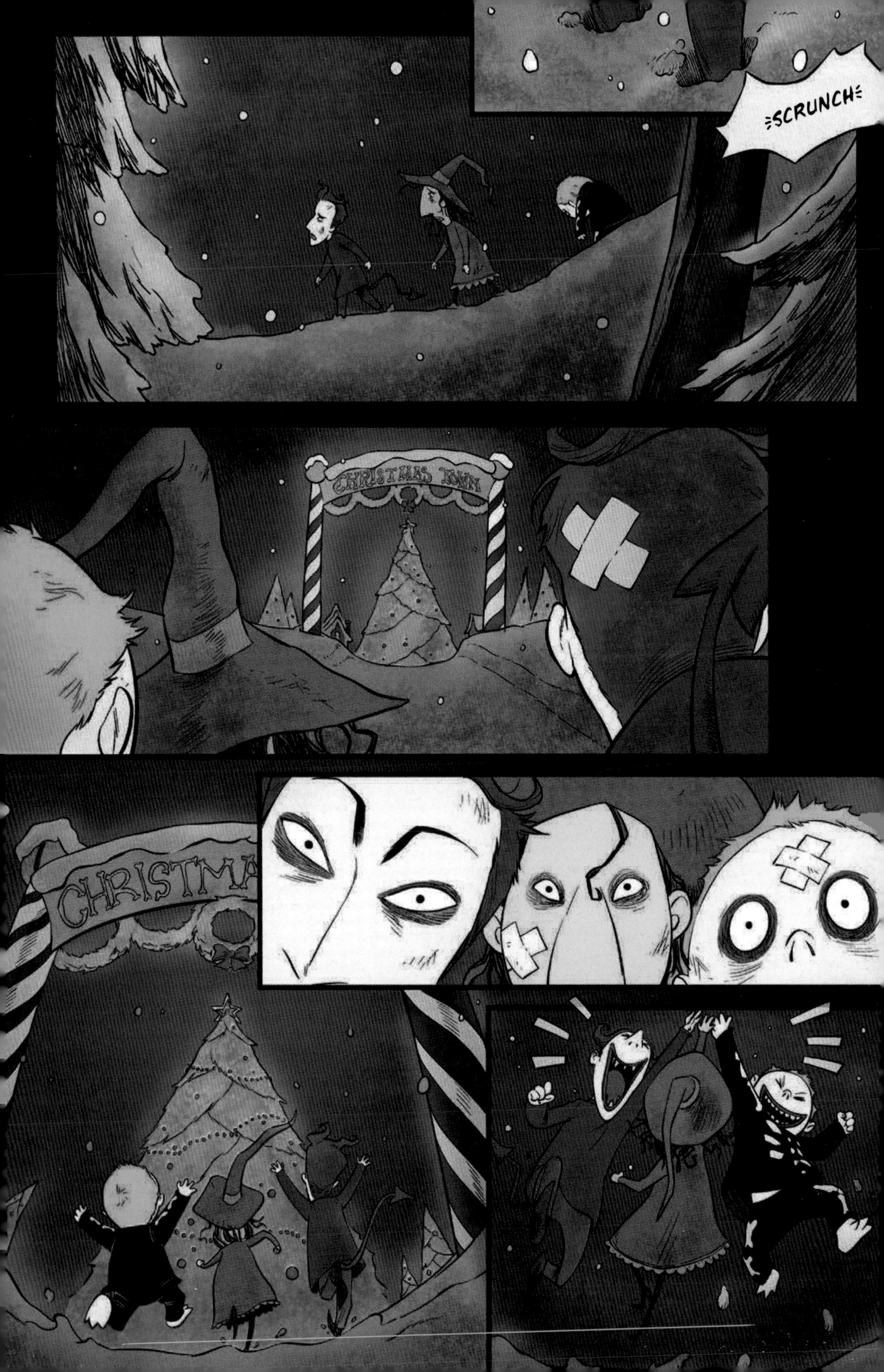
SCRUNCH
CHRISTMAS TOWN
CHRISTMA

GULP
WOOF

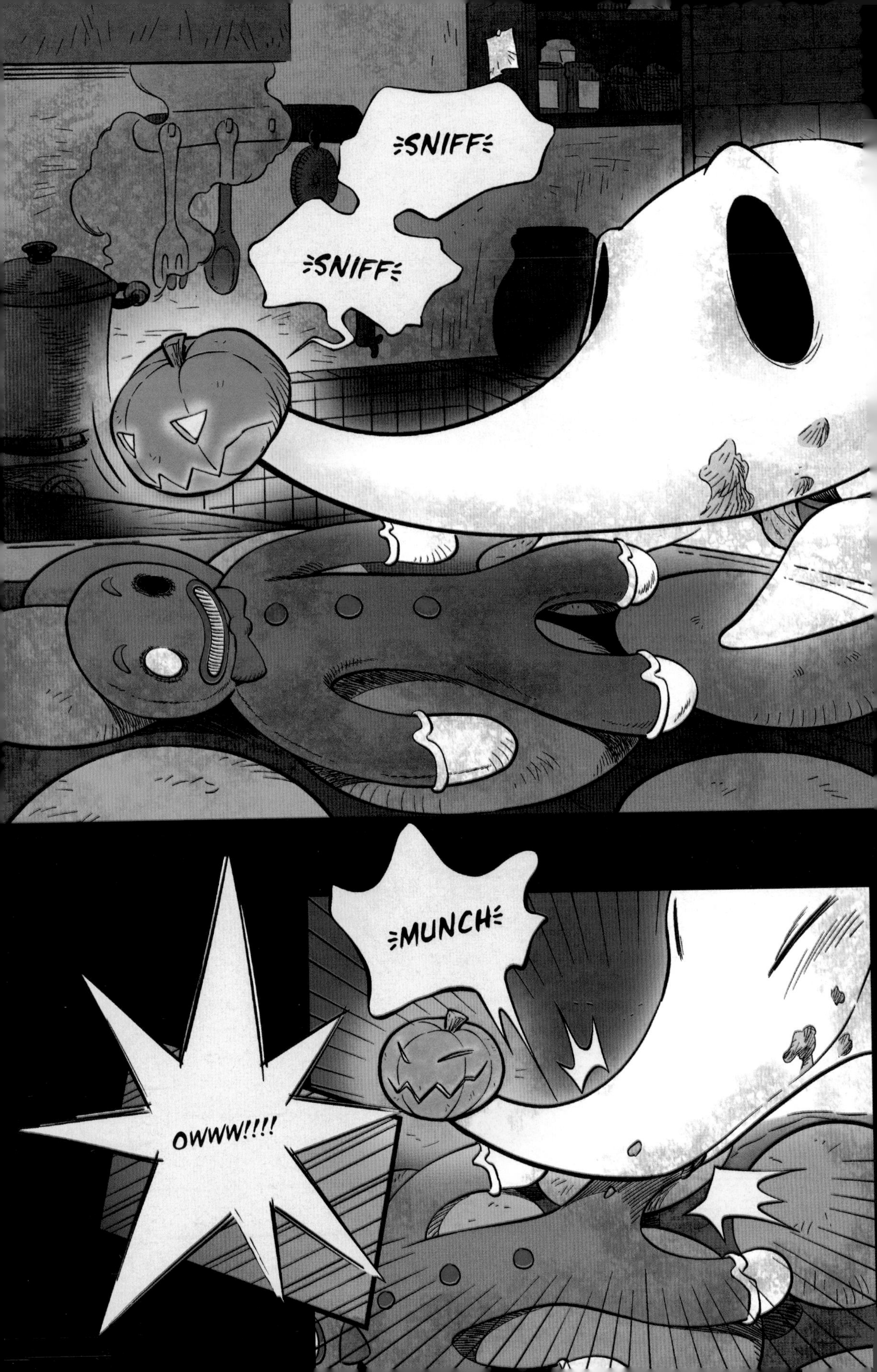
SNIFF
SNIFF
MUNCH
OWWW!!!!

THAT HURTS!
ABUSE!
HOW DARE YOU ABUSE ME!
YOU CHOCOLATE EATER!
THIS MEANS WAR!!
HOPE YOU GET A STOMACH-ACHE!

OH, YOU THINK YOU CAN GET OFF THAT EASILY?
BOIL
BOIL
GRAB
WHACK
YANK
YANK

PUSH
PUSH
ARRFFF!
SLAM
WOOOF
TO BE CONTINUED

Disney
Tim Burton's The Nightmare Before Christmas
Zero's Journey
COVER GALLERY

ISSUE #0

FREE COMIC BOOK DAY EDITION (KIYOSHI ARAI)

ISSUE #1

MAIN COVER (KIYOSHI ARAI)

ISSUE #1 - VARIANT COVER

VARIANT COVER (KEI ISHIYAMA, DAVID HUTCHISON, DAN CONNER)

ISSUE #2

MAIN COVER (KIYOSHI ARAI)

ISSUE #3

MAIN COVER (KIYOSHI ARAI)

MAIN COVER (KIYOSHI ARAI)

GRAPHIC NOVEL #1

MAIN COVER (KIYOSHI ARAI)

GRAPHIC NOVEL #1

VARIANT COVER (CAMILLA D'ERRICO)

COVER CREATION - BEHIND THE SCENES

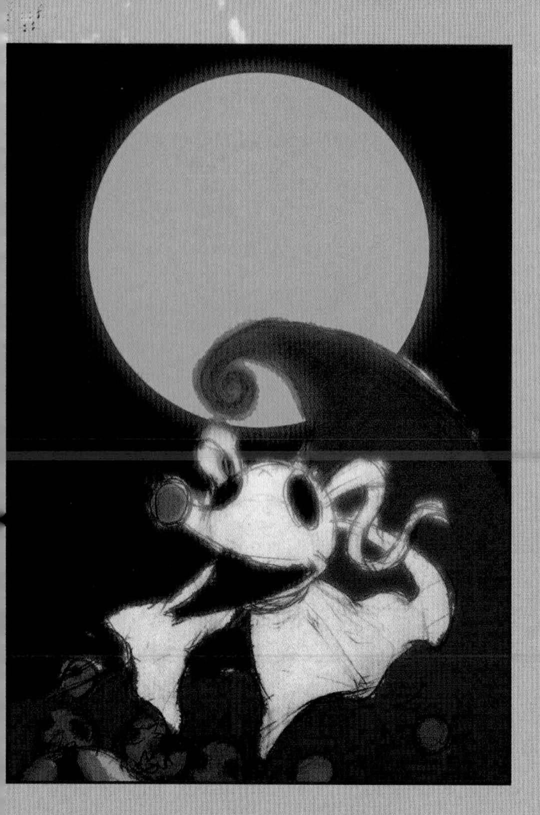

CREATING COVERS IS FUN!!

WITH THE 25TH ANNIVERSARY OF ***THE NIGHTMARE BEFORE CHRISTMAS*** STEADFASTLY APPROACHING, WE HAD LOTS OF IDEAS THAT WOULD MAKE THIS PROJECT FEEL MORE SPECIAL. HERE ARE ONLY A FEW OF THE CONCEPTS THAT THE MAIN COVER ARTIST CAME UP WITH.

"THE TOP LEFT IMAGE WAS INSPIRED BY THE KEY VISUAL FOR THE NIGHTMARE BEFORE CHRISTMAS: THE MOON, AND THE SPRILL HILL. FOR THE BOTTOM LEFT COVER, I USED A SIMPLE EYE-CATCHING APPROACH THAT FEATURES ONLY ZERO. I DREW THE BOTTOM RIGHT IMAGE TO BE THE FIRST OF FIVE COVERS THAT COULD BE ARRANGED SIDE-BY-SIDE TO CREATE ONE IMAGE. I LIKED CREATING ALL OF THEM!"

-- KIYOSHI ARAI, THE MAIN COVER ARTIST

COVER CREATION - BEHIND THE SCENES

ADDITIONAL SKETCHES!!

HERE ARE SOME BONUS COVER ART SKETCHES FROM CAMILLA D'ERRICO, AN AMAZINGLY TALENTED ARTIST WE ADORED WORKING WITH. WE WANTED TO SHOWCASE HER CREATIVE TAKE ON ***TIM BURTON'S THE NIGHTMARE BEFORE CHRISTMAS*** WORLD.

COVER CREATION - BEHIND THE SCENES

ISSUE #1 VARIANT COVER -- SKETCH

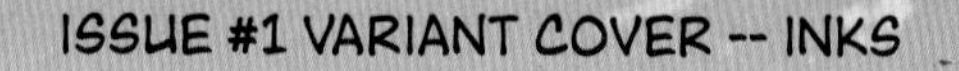

ISSUE #1 -- MAIN COVER (SKETCH 1)

ISSUE #1 -- MAIN COVER (SKETCH 2)

COVER CREATION - BEHIND THE SCENES

ISSUE #0 SKETCHES

ISSUE #0 ALTERNATE COVER

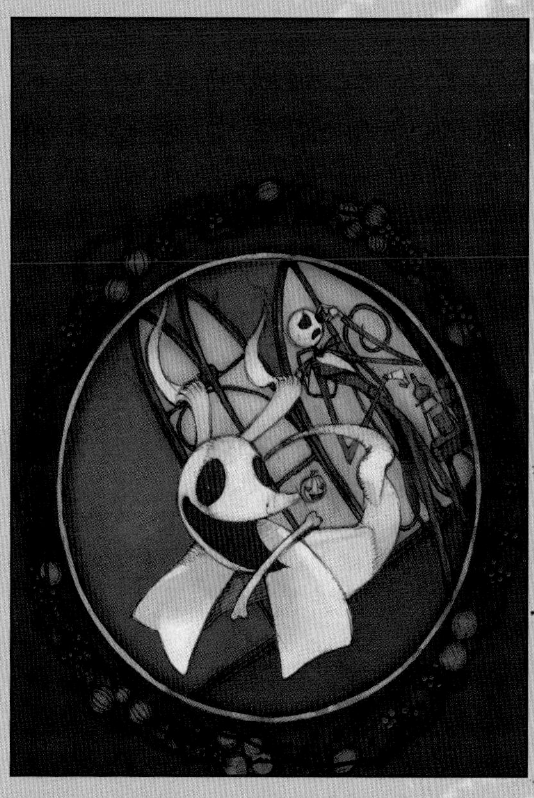

ISSUE #3 ALTERNATE COVER

ISSUE #4 COVER SKETCH

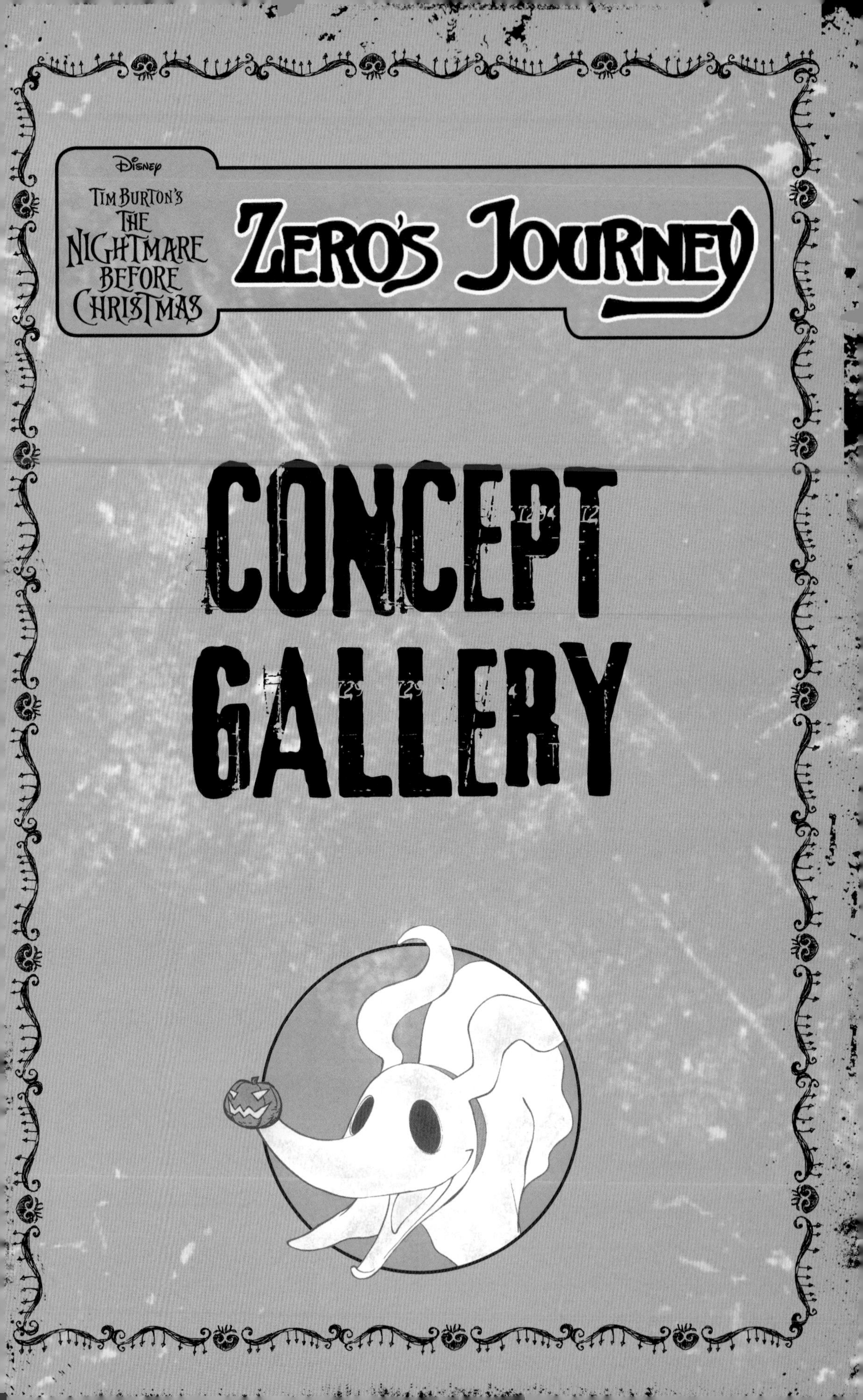
Disney
Tim Burton's
The Nightmare Before Christmas
Zero's Journey
CONCEPT
GALLERY

ZERO

CONCEPT

TAKE A PEEK AT SOME OF THE NEVER BEFORE RELEASED CHARACTER CONCEPTS AND LOCATION SKETCHES! WE COLLABORATED WITH A TEAM OF DEDICATED JAPANESE AND AMERICAN ARTISTS TO CREATE THE ART FOR THIS SPECTACULAR MANGA ADVENTURE!

KIYOSHI ARAI

KEI ISHIYAMA

JACK SKELLINGTON

CONCEPT (KIYOSHI ARAI)

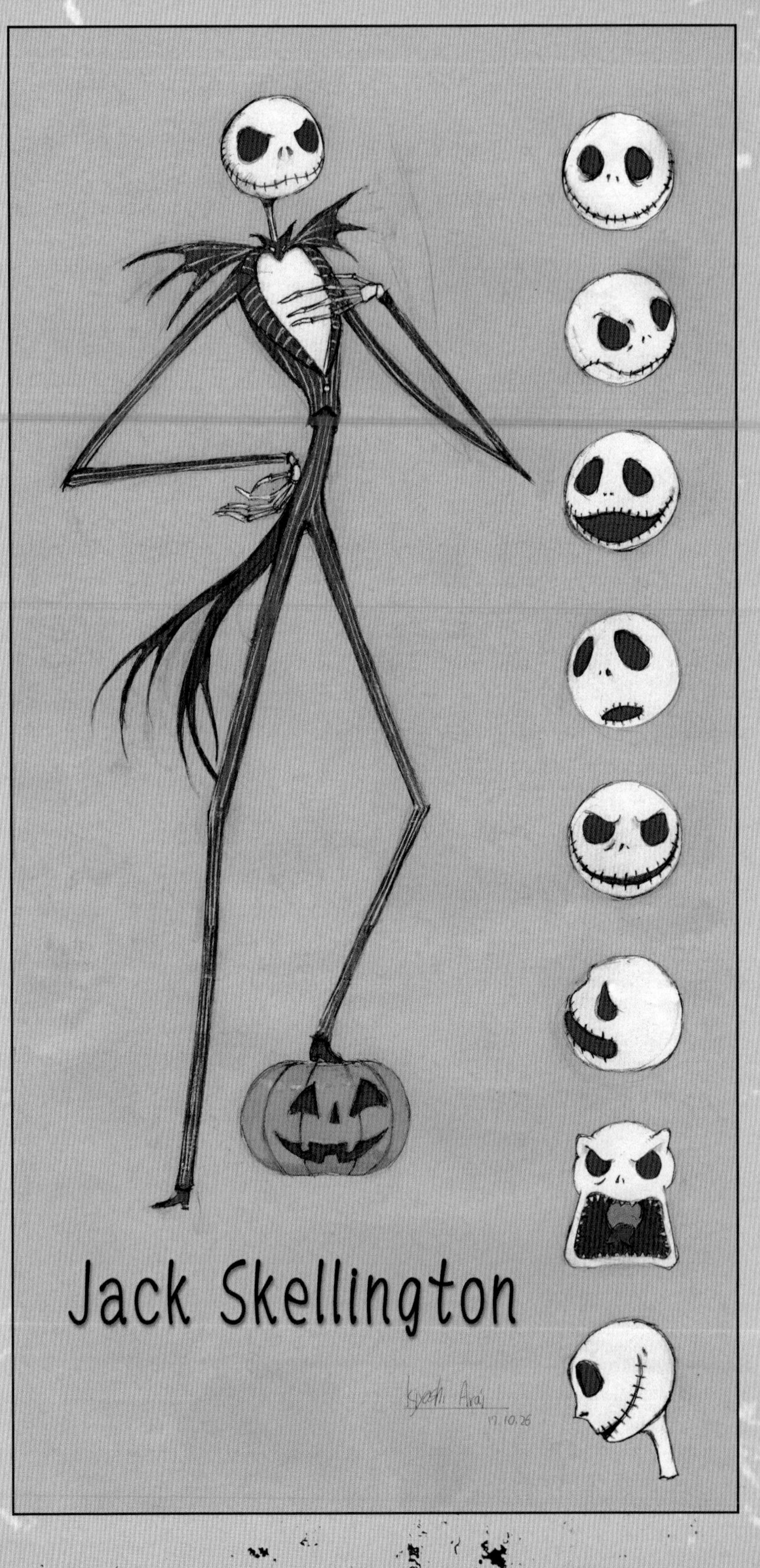

JACK & ZERO

CONCEPT (KEI ISHIYAMA)

HOWLY

CONCEPT (KIYOSHI ARAI)

JOUELLE

CONCEPT (KIYOSHI ARAI)

LOCATION CONCEPTS

JACK'S ROOM (KIYOSHI ARAI)

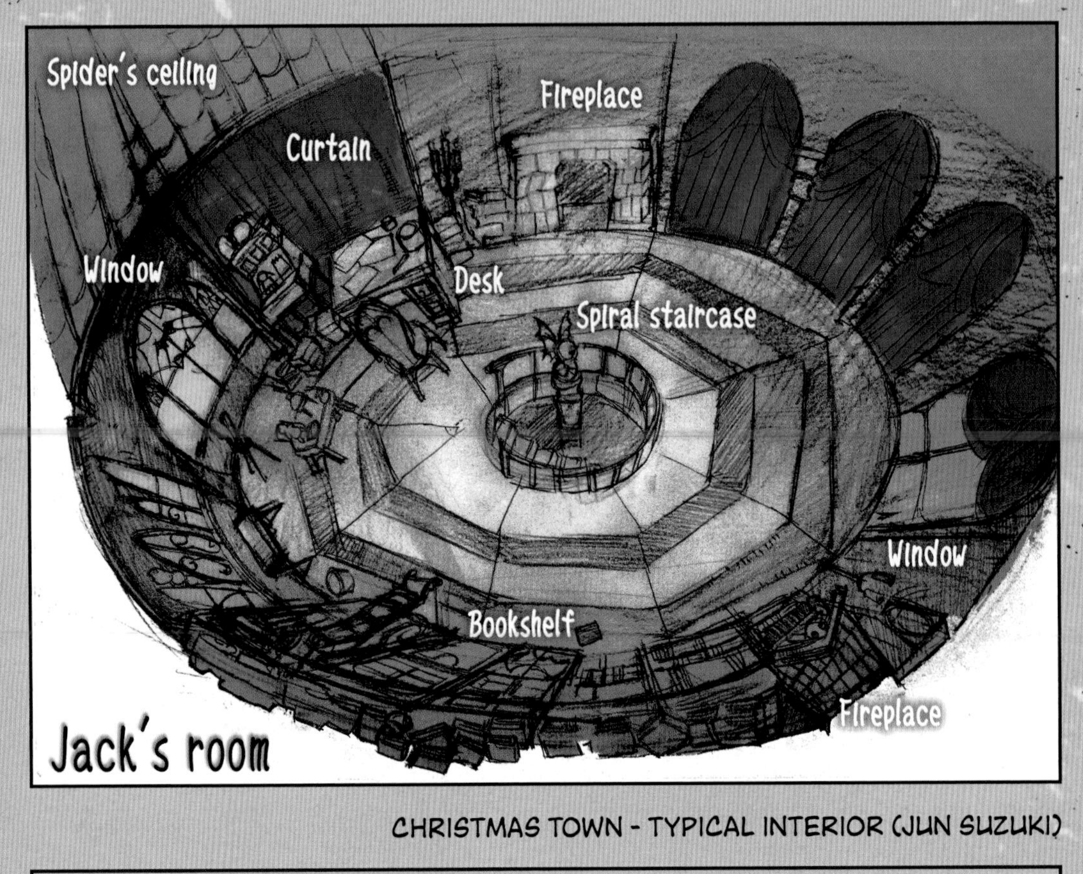

CHRISTMAS TOWN - TYPICAL INTERIOR (JUN SUZUKI)

LOCATION CONCEPTS

JOUELLE'S ROOM (KIYOSHI ARAI)

ZERO IS LOST...
CAN HE FIND HIS
WAY HOME?

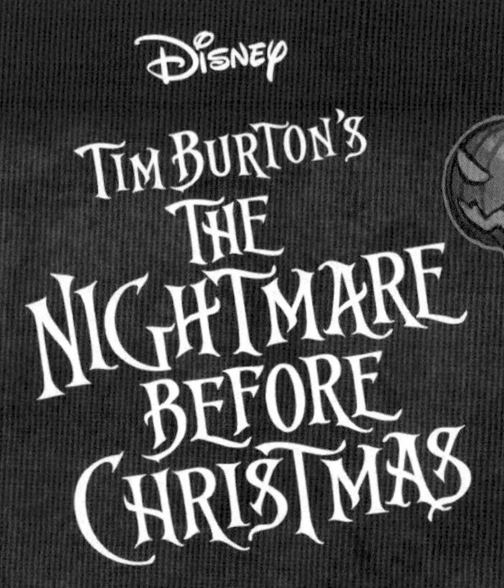

ZERO'S JOURNEY

© Disney

Disney Tim Burton's The Nightmare Before Christmas: Zero's Journey Graphic Novel Volume 1

Original Characters by - Tim Burton
Story by - D.J. Milky
Main Printing Cover by - Kiyoshi Arai
Variant Cover by - Camilla d'Errico
Variant Cover Colors by - Amanda Duarte
Character Design - Kiyoshi Arai
Concept Art - Kiyoshi Arai & Jun Suzuki
Storyboards and Pencils by - Kei Ishiyama
Inks by - David Hutchison
Colors by - Dan Conner
Issue #0 Color Flats by - Mary Bellamy and Tony Galvan
Issue #1 - #4 Color Flats by - Patricia Krmpotich

Editorial Associate - Janae Young
Marketing Associate - Kae Winters
Digital Media Coordinator - Rico Brenner-Quiñonez
Technology and Digital Media Assistant - Phillip Hong
Translator - Rie Sato Sakuraba
Editorial Coordinator - Daisuke Fukada
Operations Coordinator d'Errico Studios Ltd. - Tasha Zimich
Editor - Stu Levy
Graphic Designer - Phillip Hong
Retouching and Lettering - Vibrraant Publishing Studio
Editor-in-Chief & Publisher - Stu Levy

A TOKYOPOP® Manga

TOKYOPOP and are trademarks or registered trademarks of TOKYOPOP Inc.

TOKYOPOP inc.
5200 W Century Blvd
Suite 705
Los Angeles, CA 90045 USA

E-mail: info@TOKYOPOP.com
Come visit us online at www.TOKYOPOP.com

www.facebook.com/TOKYOPOP
www.twitter.com/TOKYOPOP
www.youtube.com/TOKYOPOPTV
www.pinterest.com/TOKYOPOP
www.instagram.com/TOKYOPOP
TOKYOPOP.tumblr.com

©2019 Disney
All Rights Reserved

All rights reserved. No portion of this book may be reproduced or transmitted in any form or by any means without written permission from the copyright holders. This manga is a work of fiction. Any resemblance to actual events or locales or persons, living or dead, is entirely coincidental.

Scholastic Print Edition: 978-1-4278-6172-6

First TOKYOPOP Printing: June 2019

10 9 8 7 6 5 4 3 2 1

Printed in CANADA

Don't Be Like ZERO and Get LOST!

You Read Manga From Right to Left and Top to Bottom From Each Panel!